FACES PLACES PEOPLE too

by Tessa Brusven

Tellwell Talent
www.tellwell.ca

ISBN
978-0-2288-1231-9 (Hardcover)
978-0-2288-1230-2 (Paperback)
978-0-2288-1232-6 (eBook)

Keep your eyes peeled for this little beauty. Miss Ladybird
Beetle makes an appearance on every page!

It's so exciting, can't you see, there's endless possibility!

Catching bugs and riding bikes,

Double-Dutch and flying kites.

Planting flowers, baking cakes,

licking lollies,
tummy aches.

Flying rocket ships to Mars and dancing 'round a sky of stars.

The most important

thing you see,

is sharing

POSITIVITY

Maybe just to give a smile
to someone whose been sad a while.

Changing hearts from should to could,

show the world that there IS good!

That even though there's lots of

HATE

there's no need to participate.

Instead we choose
to put on Love,

the Love that comes
from up above.

LOVE

Every day is something new, let positivity shine through.
Faces, places, people too, all need love.

It starts with you!

THE END

To...
those whose dreams have not been tried
To those who fail to see,
That if you put your mind to it
There's nothing you can't be.

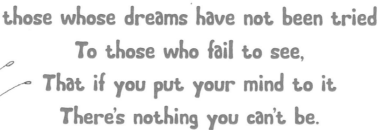

This book's for you, I hope you learn
That life has so much more,
Than working at that numbing job
The one that is a bore.

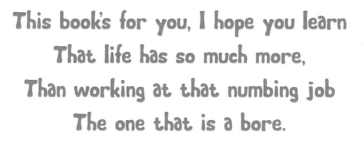

Find the things that make you feel
Excitement, joy and pain,
Take those things and wait for God
To present His perfect way.

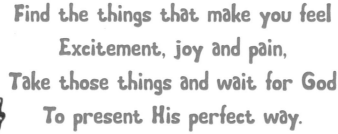

ACKOWLEDGEMENTS

What a journey this has been... Hundreds of hours, conversations, revisions, late nights and doubts later,
and now I have something that I pray will leave people more hopeful, optimistic and ultimately loved.

I want to start by thanking my family.
Momma, thank you for continually showing me love and grace when I was frustrated, stressed and hard to love.
Daddy'o, thank you for letting me bounce idea after idea off of you and for all your creative input.
Brother, when I felt as if I wasn't good enough, you reaffirmed me of my capabilities,
vision and gave me the confidence to finish. Thank you.
Aunty Danielle and Uncle Greg, thank you for your continual support, ideas and proofreads.

Grandparents, you guys were the best cheerleaders a girl could ask for, thank you!

Next, I want to thank all my friends and mentors that gave me advice, skills, confidence and encouragement.

Jessica Evans, Tom Garfield, Natalie Germain, Pat and Rosie Greenfield, Katie Meyer, Jessica Musika and Hannah Owens.

And to everyone else that ever gave me a pep talk, word of encouragement
or constructive feedback, I appreciate you and thank you!

"Not unto us, **O LORD**, not unto us, but unto thy name give glory."